Where Is Bear?

For Chloe + Connor,
with a big bear hug!

Lœlia Nunn

Where Is Bear?

written by Lesléa Newman

illustrated by Valeri Gorbachev

Gulliver Books * Harcourt, Inc.

Orlando   Austin   New York   San Diego   Toronto   London

Manufactured in China

Who wants to go play hide-and-seek?
Everyone hide. Bunny, don't peek!

With eyes shut tight so she can't see,
Bunny counts out, "One, two, three..."

Fox sneaks behind a fallen log.
Oops! She almost sat on Frog.

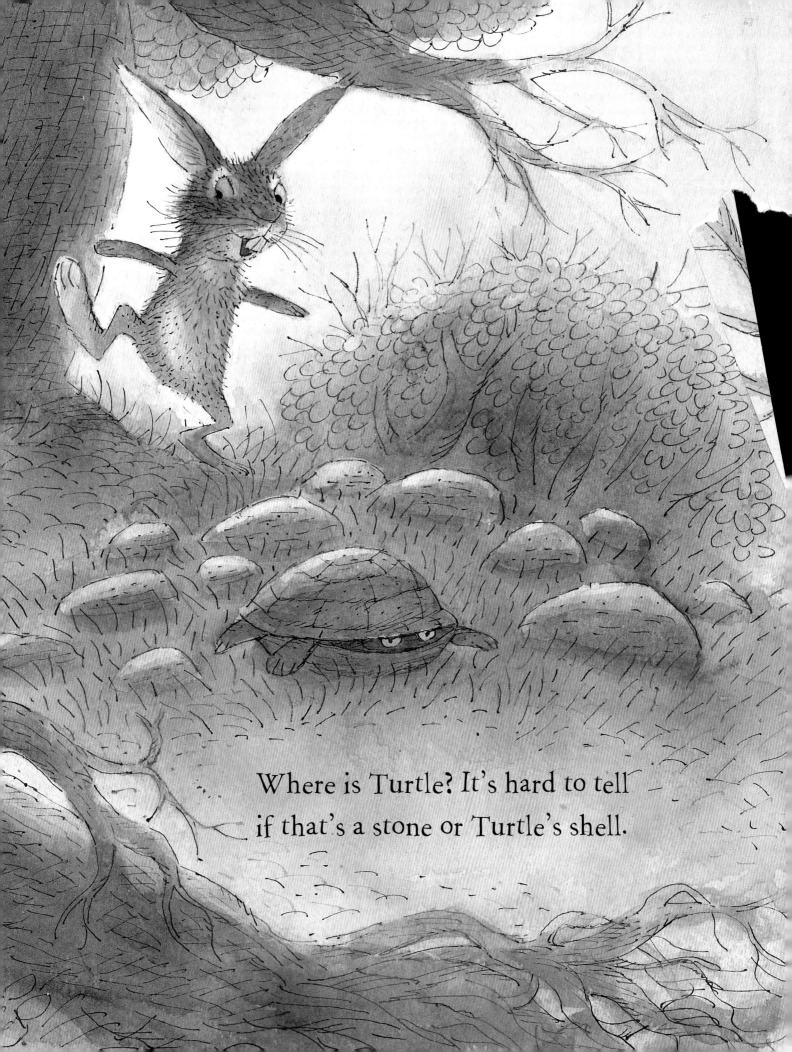

Where is Turtle? It's hard to tell
if that's a stone or Turtle's shell.

Can Chipmunk fit behind that twig?
I don't think so. She's too big.

Skunk digs out a great big hole
and hides beside a friendly Mole.

Ant and Beetle slip below
the big black shiny wing of Crow.

Ladybug flies across the lake
to hide beneath a rock with Snake.

Now all are found except for Bear.
No one sees him anywhere.

Beetle asks, "Where can he be?
We've got to find Bear instantly!"

Frog leaps on a pile of rocks
to look for Bear along with Fox.

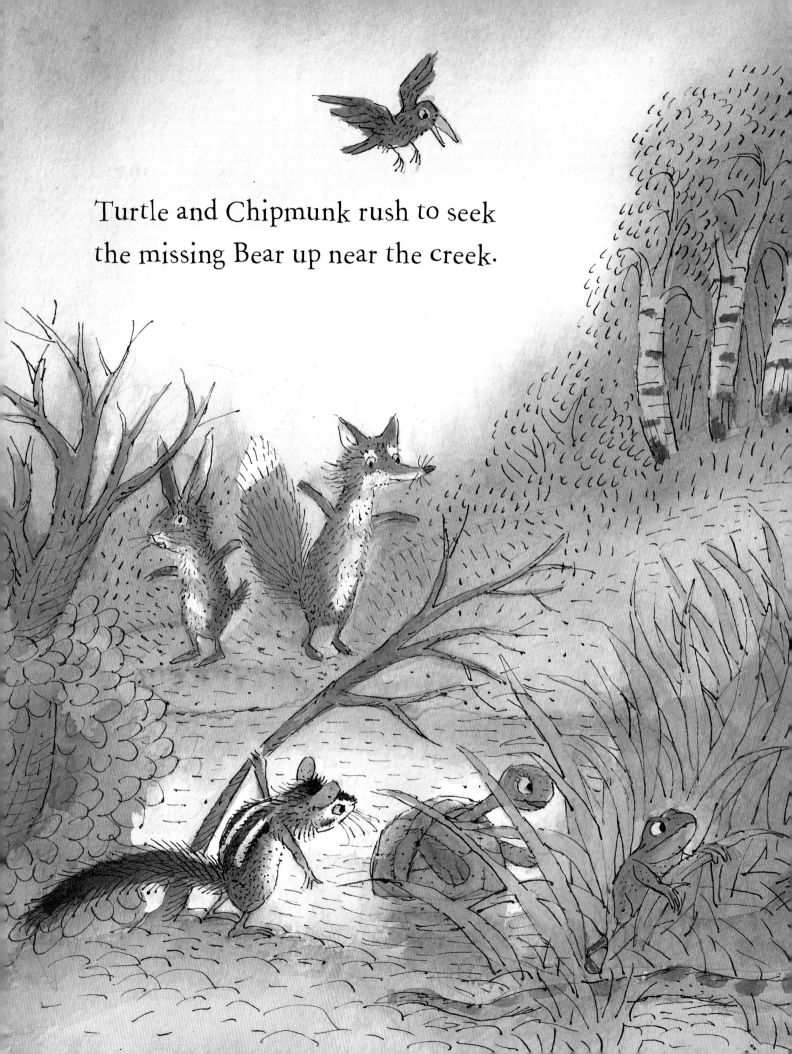

Turtle and Chipmunk rush to seek
the missing Bear up near the creek.

Mole hurries to catch up with Skunk,
who peers behind an old tree trunk.

Ladybug rides on Snake's long tail
as they explore a curvy trail.

Ant and Beetle search the weeds.
Crow flies high above the reeds.

The animals all gather round.
"Oh no," cries Snake. "Bear's still not found."

Turtle, Skunk, and Bunny shout,
"Come out, Bear. Come out, come out!"

Could Bear be hurt? Could Bear be sick?

Or could this be an old Bear trick?

There's one place left where Bear might be,
but no one wants to look and see.

It's cold and damp and dark as night.
It fills the animals with fright.

Who is feeling very brave?
Who will go inside this cave?

Bunny says, "We'll go as one.
That's the way it must be done."

Who's that sleeping over there?

Wake up now, you silly Bear!

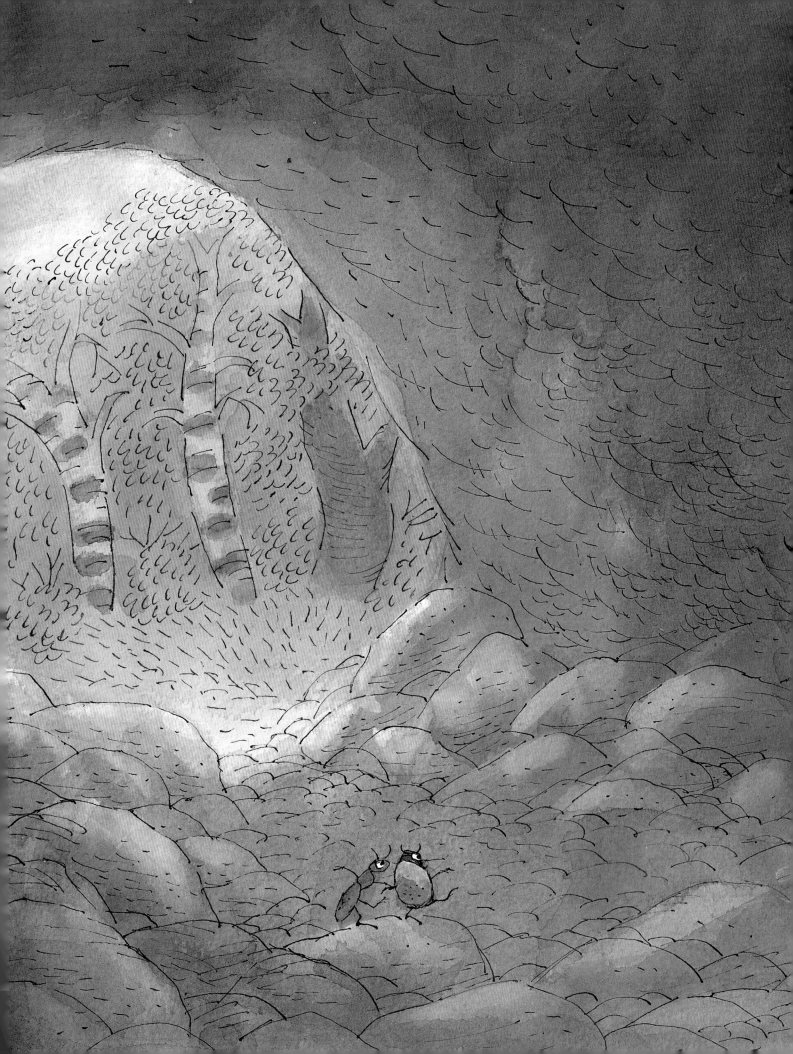

Crow and Fox give Bear a hug.
"And here's a kiss," says Ladybug.

Bear shouts, "Who wants to play again?"
He shuts his eyes to count to ten.

"One, two, three, four..."

That sleepy Bear begins to snore!

For Judy O.: "Come out, come out,
wherever you are!" —L. N.

For Kate and Scott — -V. G.

Text copyright © 2004 by Lesléa Newman
Illustrations copyright © 2004 by Valeri Gorbachev

www.HarcourtBooks.com

Library of Congress Cataloging-in-Publication Data
Newman, Lesléa.
Where is Bear?/written by Lesléa Newman; illustrated by Valeri Gorbachev.
p. cm.
"Gulliver Books."
Summary: The animals in the forest are playing hide-and-seek, but none
of them can find Bear anywhere.
[1. Hide-and-seek—Fiction. 2. Bears—Fiction. 3. Animals—Fiction.
4. Stories in rhyme.] I. Gorbachev, Valeri, ill. II. Title.
PZ8.3.N4655Wh 2004
[E]—dc22   2003019439
ISBN 0-15-204936-3

First edition
H G F E D C B A

The illustrations in this book were done in pen-and-ink and watercolors.
The display type and text type were set in P22 Garamouche.
Color separations by Colourscan Co. Pte. Ltd., Singapore
Manufactured by South China Printing Company, Ltd., China
This book was printed on totally chlorine-free Stora Enso Matte paper.
Production supervision by Sandra Grebenar and Pascha Gerlinger
Designed by Scott Piehl